Sins of the Flesh

A Dark Sins novella

Gluttony

By Stacey Broadbent

Published by Stacey Broadbent
Copyright 2019 © Stacey Broadbent

Originally published as part of the
Witching Hour: Vices and Virtues anthology

Licence Notes

Proofreading by Spell Bound
Cover image from Deposit Photos
Cover design by Stacey Broadbent
ISBN: 978-0-473-50511-0
        978-0-473-50512-7

Sins of the Flesh

Contents

Author's Note

The characters in this story are from New Zealand, therefore UK spelling and terms have been used. Please remember these are not errors, it's just the way we do things here.

Please also note, this story contains scenes of a graphic nature.

Chapter One

Saturday, 7th September, 2019

IT WAS A BALMY SPRING EVENING when I first discovered a taste for human flesh. It was a happy accident really. After having my heart broken one too many times, I'd abstained from any type of physical relationship with a man for years, so when one fell in my lap, it came as quite the surprise…

Perusing the shelves at my local supermarket, we both reached for the same bottle of wine. Our fingers touched, sending a tingle of excitement coursing through my body. I stepped back, apologising profusely, but not before getting a glimpse of his gorgeous blue eyes. "So sorry, you take it." I then bowed, tucking my head into my chest so he couldn't see my eyes roll at my awkwardness.

The rumble of his laughter made me pause, my eyes peeking up through my hair. "I think there's enough for the both of us." He winked, handing me a bottle then reaching back to grab another for himself. He opened his mouth as if to say something then quickly shut it again with a shake of his head as he turned to walk away. He took two steps before spinning back to face me. "This may be forward of me, but I don't suppose you'd be interested in joining me for a tipple?"

"Ah… I don't know…"

He thrust his hand out towards me. "Where are my manners? Of course you don't want a drink with a stranger. Let's remedy that. Mark's the name. And you are?"

Slipping my tiny hand into his, I inwardly shuddered at the softness of his skin on mine. "P-Piper," I stuttered, slowly bringing my eyes up to meet his. His grin broadened, and I got a glimpse of a dimple in his left cheek. Oh how I loved a dimple. There's something so endearing about them.

"Nice to meet you, Piper." He nodded towards the bottle in my hand. "And can I say, you have excellent taste in wine."

Perhaps it was the ever-present grin on his face, or the sparkle in his ocean-blue eyes that had me letting down my guard. "You may." I glanced at the basket slung over his arm. "Camembert and crackers. Someone's letting their hair down tonight."

Without missing a beat, he flicked his luscious locks from his face. "You bet I am!" He leaned in close to whisper in my ear. "Wine, snacks and a 1000-piece puzzle with my name on it." He stepped back, his eyes alight. "Irresistible, I know."

The snort that came out of my nose when I laughed took me by surprise, and I quickly brought my hand up to hide my embarrassment. Anticipating my move, he grasped my hand, pulling it from my face. "Don't hide. You have a beautiful smile." And just like that, I was putty in his hands. "Have a drink with me?"

He looked so hopeful. How could I possibly resist? It was just one drink, after all. "Sure, why not?" His face lit up like a kid on Christmas day, and I couldn't help but grin back at him.

With our purchases in our hands, we walked out to the parking lot, stopping at the edge. "Where are you parked?" he asked, taking hold of my bag.

"Just over there." I pointed to my white Honda Civic just two rows over.

"I'll walk you to your car."

Nodding, I stepped onto the asphalt, leading the way. What was the correct protocol for things like this? I'd been out of the game for so long, I had no idea how I was meant to behave. Do I follow him? Do we go together? Should I ask for his number? Do I go home and get changed first?

"So, about that drink?" Mark's voice interrupted my mini meltdown, his grin setting me at ease once again. I'd been so preoccupied with my thoughts, I hadn't even noticed we were standing beside my car and he was waiting for me to open it. He stood, staring at me expectantly as I rummaged around for my keys.

"Ah, here they are!" I said a little too loudly, jingling them in the air. "Let me just open this up…" A beep sounded as I pressed the button on the fob, and the boot popped open. "You can put the bag in there."

He placed it down carefully then turned back to me. "Piper?"

"Mmm?"

"Drink?" His grin was almost boyish, and I could feel the heat rising in my cheeks as I followed his tongue as he licked his lips.

"Uh, yeah." I blinked, forcing my eyes to shift from his mouth. "Sorry, I'm out of practise. How do we," I gestured between the two of us, "do this?"

He threw his head back and laughed. "You're doing just fine. How about you follow me back to mine, and we can get to know each other over a bottle of wine and a box of cardboard shapes?"

Cocking my head to the side, I wondered if it was a good idea to be somewhere less public with this man I barely knew. He seemed nice enough, but my track record proved I wasn't much of a judge of character.

"Or we could go somewhere else, if you'd rather. I understand if you'd prefer to be somewhere less… intimate."

The nice girl in me who was always eager to please and not disappoint quickly jumped to attention. "No, don't be silly. Your place sounds nice. Lead the way." *You only live once, right?*

Chapter Two

WE PULLED UP OUTSIDE a modern-looking townhouse with perfectly manicured lawns and gardens. Mark quickly strode over to my car, offering me a hand to climb out, and grabbing the bag, like a true gentleman. He ushered me through the gate with a hand to the small of my back, and butterflies flitted about in my stomach at such a sweet gesture. It had been much too long since I'd enjoyed the touch of a good man.

He shook the keys once before inserting them in the lock and opening the door. When we stepped inside, he took my coat and hung it by the door on one of those old-school coat racks, then directed me through to the kitchen where he set the bags down on the counter. "Wine?" he asked, holding the bottle in one hand, while he reached into the cupboard for glasses.

"Mmm, please." I wandered around the room, mesmerised by the artwork on his walls. Streaks of red and black, smatterings of pink and white, such bold colours and vivid imagery. "You paint?"

"Me?" He pointed a finger at his chest before belting out a laugh. "No, though I'm flattered you think I'm capable of such things. Not an artistic bone in this body, I'm afraid." Walking around the counter, he handed me my glass. "To new friends." We clinked before taking a sip of the warm, crimson liquid.

I closed my eyes, savouring the taste on my tongue. "Mmm. I needed that."

"Rough day?" He led me over to the couch, placing our glasses on the coffee table.

"Busy. Nothing to write home about." I stretched my neck as I sat beside him.

His warm hands clamped down on my shoulders. "May I?" he asked as he began slowly kneading the knots from my aching muscles.

"Mmm, that feels good." I closed my eyes, allowing my head to loll backwards while his fingers worked their magic on me.

"How does that feel now?" The husky tone of his voice stirred emotions I hadn't felt in a while. It scared me how quickly I was falling under his spell. Scooting forward, I perched on the edge of the couch, taking another gulp of wine. "Ah… I believe you mentioned a puzzle?"

"Oh, yeah." He smiled, rubbing his hands together. "Are you sure you don't mind? I know it's not something you'd normally do on a first date."

"No? You don't lure women back here to help you slot your piece into theirs?" I wiggled my eyebrows at him, surprising myself. Either the wine was stronger than I remembered, or he'd cast some sort of voodoo on me. I wasn't normally so bold.

His laughter boomed from his chest again, and his eyes twinkled. "You're funny. I like that." He stood, reaching underneath us to pull out a thin black suitcase-type thing. "Puzzle case," he said, laying it on the table. A long zip ran around the outer edge. Inside was a suede lining with two matching boards for putting spare pieces on. I could see he'd made a start on it, having the outside edges already put together. "I started without you, sorry. If I'd known a lovely lady would give up her Saturday night to help me, I'd have waited." He winked.

"I think I can forgive you for that. Where's the box? What picture are we making?" I started grabbing pieces that looked as though they might match. It was hard to tell though, so many looked the same.

"Ah." He tapped his forehead. "I prefer to do it without the picture. Makes it more interesting." He handed me a handful of pieces from a plastic bag he had stashed. "Let's get some more spread out on the spare boards. I'll grab us another wine."

The first glass was already making me feel lightheaded, but I needed the Dutch courage. "Superb." I was busy trying to slot two red and white pieces together when he came back in carrying a tray with our glasses and an array of snacks.

"Thought we could use a little nibble while we work." He set the tray down on a side table, dragging it closer. "You have to try the jerky. I make it myself."

"Really? Aren't you the clever one?" I was suitably impressed. Not only did he have a nice home and great choice in wine, but he could also work his way around a kitchen! What more could you ask for in a man?

I popped a piece of shrivelled-up meat into my mouth, chewing slowly. "Mmm, this is really good," I mumbled around my mouthful.

"Isn't it, though? The trick is in the way you cure it. You must take your time. Maybe I could show you later?" He sounded hopeful, once again giving him an air of boyish charm.

"I'd like that." I took a large gulp of wine to wash down the salty meat. "What's it made of? Beef?"

"It's kind of a… sausage. I work with whatever I can get my hands on really." Topping my glass up even more, he watched me with interest. "I think you'd enjoy the process. It's… cathartic."

Chapter Three

"WHERE ARE WE GOING?" With a bottle of wine and then some in my system, I stumbled down the hall after him, desperate to see his surprise.

"I told you, I want to show you something." He grinned back at me, his eyes darting to a space above my head as he reached for my hand. "Come on, slowpoke." We stopped outside a closed door, and I peered up at him in question.

"What's in there?" I whispered, excited by the cloak-and-daggers mystery.

"Shhh." He held a finger to my lips. "You'll scare him."

I scrunched my brow in confusion. "Him? Did you kidnap someone?" The very thought of this man before me being capable of kidnapping someone was absurd. A sudden urge to giggle bubbled up and I clamped my hand across my mouth, though it didn't stop the sounds from squeezing out between my fingers.

Without answering me, he turned the handle and opened the door. The room was dark but for a tiny sliver of moonlight peeking through the curtain of a small rectangular window near the ceiling. In the middle of the room was a king size bed, and strapped in the centre, was a naked man. He wore a blindfold and nothing else.

"H-hello?" he spoke in a hushed whisper.

Mark slipped into the room, making his way to the bed. "Shh, it's time." He ran a finger along the man's foot and up the side of his body, eliciting a whimper. I watched in fascination as his flaccid cock kicked and began to rise. "I'm going to take this off now. Be a good boy and keep your eyes closed." He tugged at the fabric covering the man's eyes.

My heart thundered in my chest as I turned to Mark with a questioning look. Trailing his finger back down the length of the man, he locked eyes with me, beckoning me to him. Before I could even think about it, my feet began to move of their own accord. Perhaps because it had been so long since I'd been with a man, or perhaps it was the thrill of the unknown, I couldn't tell you. All I know is, I wanted to please him.

When I was standing by the corner of the bed, he leaned in to whisper in my ear. "He's here for you."

"For me?" I pointed at my chest. "But… how…" What he was saying didn't make sense. We only just met. How could he have known I'd come home with him?

Walking around to stand behind me, he cupped my shoulders in his large hands. The feel of him standing so close to me, his hands on my body, made me lose my train of thought. I leaned back against him, inhaling through my nose as I closed my eyes. I had no idea what was going on, but it was churning up all these strange emotions inside. The heady scent of arousal filled my nostrils, sending a powerful jolt to my core.

"That's it." His lips brushed the sensitive part below my ear, making me shiver. "Go on, taste him." He gave a gentle push on my shoulders, leading me to stand between the legs of the naked man whose member pulsed in front of me.

I'd never done anything like this before, and the thrill was like nothing I'd ever experienced before. I climbed onto the bed tentatively, my hands braced on either side of his knees. When I peeked back over my shoulder, Mark nodded, his eyes hooded as he licked his lips. Lowering my head, I ran my tongue along the man's inner thigh while he trembled beneath me.

Taste him.

With those words in my head, I circled my tongue around the tip of his shaft, tasting the saltiness of his excitement. He sucked in a sharp breath, his muscles tensing against his bindings as he moaned. It was enough to spur me on, eager to please both men. With my hand around his cock, I pumped once, twice, before wrapping my lips around the tip in an intimate kiss.

"That's it. How does he taste?"

"Mmmm," I hummed around his member, slowly sinking him further into my mouth. Mark placed his hands on my arse, gently kneading, turning me on even more. I pushed against his hands, encouraging him to continue his slow torment as his fingers drifted ever closer to my throbbing need.

When his hand left me, I whimpered at the loss of his touch, begging for his return. Seconds later, I was shocked by the sharp sting of his hand on my soft flesh, jolting me forward. My jaw clamped down involuntarily, and the coppery taste of blood filled my mouth as the naked man beneath me cried out in agony.

"Fuuuuuuuck!" he screamed, his arms pulling against his restraints before he passed out.

Chapter Four

"HOW DOES HE TASTE NOW, PIPER?" Mark leaned over me, his chest pressed into my back. "I knew you'd be good at this. As soon as I saw you, I knew." He reached forward, running a finger through the blood pooling around the man's groin.

I moved the flesh around in my mouth, running my tongue over the severed end. My teeth had slid through his tender member like the perfect tool, as if they were made for tearing human flesh. Testing just how far I could go, I bit down, the delicate tissue shredding in my mouth as I chewed. I should've been scared by my own actions; this wasn't normal behaviour, but instead, I found myself wanting more. Dipping my head to the open wound, I lapped at the pooling blood, strangely aroused by the warm liquid as it flowed down my throat. It was intoxicating, like a drug. I felt invincible as I sat there between his legs, feeding on him.

Mark chuckled, the sound rumbling through me. "Tut tut, gluttony is a sin, you know? Save some for later."

I turned to face him, blood smearing my face and coating my teeth. "Sorry, it's just so good. I've never had anything like it before." I pulled my sleeve across my mouth, wiping away the evidence of my feast.

"Ah, little one, you have so much more to learn." He brushed a stray hair behind my ear. "You can't rush these things. Like a fine wine needs fermentation, flesh needs curing so that we can have a supply to last us. We can't be too greedy. People will get suspicious."

Flesh needs curing... A lightbulb went off in my head. "The jerky?" No wonder it had tasted so good.

"Yes. Would you like me to show you?"

"Yes. Teach me, please."

His eyes danced in front of me, his pleasure evident. "Come on then." He pulled back, taking my hand. Hesitant to leave my newfound love of flesh, I held back, taking one last lap of the lifeblood flowing all over the bed. "You have a thirst for it, I see." He laughed, tugging my hand. "He'll still be here when we get back." With another pull on my hand, he lead me down the hall to another closed door. "This is my cold store. I keep my meat in here to cure and dry." He pushed the door open, revealing a small room lined with shelves. To the back, large hooks hung from exposed beams in the ceiling. "First, we need to prepare the meat. We'll make up a vinegar solution in this bath." He pointed at the old claw bath sitting to the left, a ring of deep red staining the porcelain. "Then we'll rest it in a salt and spice mix in the tub over there." He spoke as if it was an everyday normal activity, as if what we were doing was acceptable. And for some reason, in my mind, it was.

I walked into the room, taking in all the tools and equipment he had lining the walls. "What are these for?" I reached up, taking hold of one of the hooks.

"These are for drying. After the salt has done its thing, we hang the meat from these hooks to dry over a few days."

"A few days?" I whined, not wanting to wait that long. Now that I had a taste, I didn't think I could go back to regular store-bought meat.

Mark barked out a laugh, throwing his head back. "Ah, I made a good choice with you, it seems." He bent over the bath, placing the plug in the hole. "Grab that cider vinegar over there." He pointed to a shelf by my head. "We'll mix that with this red wine vinegar." The crimson liquid flowed into the tub, splashing up the sides and reminding me of the way my victim's blood had sprayed across his abdomen. It was beautiful.

I did as he asked, tipping the entire bottle of cider vinegar into the bath, watering down the red and giving it an almost coppery tone. "What next?"

Handing me a butcher's cleaver, he winked. "The fun part. Now, we carve our meat."

Chapter Five

MY CLOTHES WERE ALREADY RUINED, so I didn't bother with the plastic overalls Mark had offered. I watched as he pulled his protective suit on. It looked like one of those white bee-keeping suits, with elasticated sleeves and legs, only it was made of a heavy-duty plastic, ensuring no matter could stain his clothing.

Once he was covered from head to toe, we made our way back to the bedroom where the man had slowly bled out. His eyes were closed, but his mouth still hung open in a silent scream. I took a moment to look at him, trying to get an image imprinted in my brain. Something I could look back on and remember. *He was my first.*

He was young, maybe in his twenties, with sandy-blond hair and pink, puffy lips. He had a square jaw and broad shoulders that tapered down to a thin waist with sculpted abs. An unfortunate end for such an attractive man, but I struggled to feel any remorse; my mind already compartmentalising things, keeping me from shutting down.

"Why him?" I asked, curious as to what this man had done to warrant our execution of him.

"He wanted it."

"He wanted…" I waved my hand up and down the length of the bed, "… this?"

"In a manner of speaking." Mark took hold of the sharpening steel that hung from the belt of his suit and began to swipe the cleaver back and forth. "There are sites you can go to. Places you can find people who are open to… assisted suicide."

"Why not just do it themselves?"

"Some people have certain fetishes. Things that only a handful of people are willing to offer. Being eaten alive is one such fantasy."

"Being eaten alive is a fetish now? Wow. I've lived such a sheltered life." I ran my finger through the congealing blood on his thigh. "How do you even know you have that fetish? It's not like you can do it more than once."

Mark grinned. "No, I suppose not."

"Is that always how you find them? The dark web?" My eyes followed every swipe of the blade in his hand, mesmerised by the glint of the steel.

"Not always, no. But they're less likely to put up a fight that way. Makes it cleaner." With a flick of his wrist, he spun the blade until the handle was facing me. "Here."

A thrill of excitement ran through me as I took hold of the cleaver. What we were about to do was something out of a horror movie, not something you did on a first date.

"You ready?" I nodded, and he pulled a second cleaver from his back pocket. "We'll make an incision here, and remove each leg first, then the arms."

"Okay." I watched as he sliced through the joint, getting all the way through to the bone before pulling back and bringing the blade down in a sharp arc. The bone splintered and cracked, his leg only just hanging on. One more slice and the limb was severed.

"Now, your turn." He rubbed his finger in the fresh blood, using it to draw a line for me to follow. "One fluid motion, lots of pressure. You've got this."

I did as he said, feeling the tissue give way beneath my amateur hands. When I hit the bone, the blade got lodged and I had to get Mark to help me pull it out. With his large hand wrapped around mine, we swung the cleaver down, tearing through the remaining flesh and bone. "Good," he whispered in my ear, his body pressed against my back. "You're a natural."

We continued hacking at the body, pulling limbs from him and splitting them into joints until he was just a headless torso. When we were done, our bodies shone with sweat and smatterings of congealed blood. The walls around the bed resembled some sort of macabre patchwork of various shades of red, and the bed itself was sticky with bodily fluids.

What started out as an ordinary Saturday night, had quickly turned into a bloodbath of epic proportions. I stared at the carcass, body parts strewn around it, and tried to summon a shred of repentance. But there was nothing, just a dull numbness in my head, and a longing to taste just a little bit more.

Chapter Six

Sunday, 8th September, 2019

IN THE SHADOW OF DARKNESS, before the sun began to rise, I slipped home to shower and change for a new day. It'd taken all night to prep the body, and it was now soaking in a vinegar bath, softening up. I was to meet Mark back at his place in the early afternoon so he could show me what to do next.

It was all so exciting and new. I still hadn't slept, but my skin felt tacky from the exertion, and I was in desperate need of a shower. If my clothes were anything to go by, my face was going to be a mess. I was almost scared to look at my reflection, but I forced myself to. If I was going to accept this new me, I would have to face the monster in the mirror.

With the bathroom filling with steam, I began peeling my clothes off and discarding them on the floor. Stepping over the heap, I stood in front of the mirror, staring at the bloody mess before me. I looked like I'd been dragged through a bush backwards. My hair was matted to one side of my face, while the rest was fluffed up into a bird's nest at the back. There were smudges of red on my cheeks, and dark rings under my eyes, but even so, I'd never seen them look so bright, so alive.

I felt it too. More alive than I'd ever felt. I'd spent my life following the rules, staying out of trouble and trying to protect my heart, but all I'd really succeeded in was sheltering myself. I hadn't been *living*. Not really.

With another's blood flowing through my veins, I had a new lease of life. I felt like I could do anything, *be* anything. I just had to hold onto that high. But as the water cascaded over my head, I could feel the elation slipping away, being replaced by an insatiable hunger. A need for more.

I tried to ignore it and go about my day, pretending it was just a normal Sunday morning. Drinking my bitter-tasting coffee on the porch as I watched my neighbours head off in their Sunday best on their way to church, a little voice inside my head whispered *just a little taste.*

But Mark had said we had to be careful. We didn't want to draw attention to what we were doing. *What he doesn't know won't hurt him,* the voice whispered again. *What harm could it do? It's only one person...*

My fingers curled around the mug tightly as I warred with myself. It hadn't even been 24 hours and already my self-control was waning. The urge to feed again consumed me like a freshly made vampire, and I suppose, in a way, that's what I'd become.

Throwing caution to the wind, I slipped my feet into a pair of runners and walked down the road, telling myself it was to clear my mind. But really, I was on the prowl for fresh meat. Someone vulnerable—easy prey. I had to be smart about it; it was broad daylight after all.

Every person who walked past became a possible target. In my mind's eye, I pictured a computer log for each one, listing their attributes like one of those *Terminator* movies.

Having limited knowledge on the ins and outs of cannibalism, I had no idea what the perfect body type was for consumption. Would it matter if they were male or female? Was it better if they were lean and muscular, or was a layer of padding more flavourful? How was I to choose?

Turns out, I didn't need to think about it at all. With my head bowed in defeat, I walked back home having found no one I thought would do. I was a matter of steps from my home when I was knocked off my feet by a man out for a jog. He'd been too busy flicking through the playlist on his phone to see me, and by the time we'd both looked up, it was too late. We collided, my forehead into his chin and mouth. My hands automatically went up, pressing against his chest and sending us both bouncing off each other, landing on our behinds. Apologising profusely, he offered me his hand and pulled me to my feet. The impact had left a red egg on my head and skinned my palms raw. He, however, came across a little worse for wear, sporting a newly chipped tooth, and fat, bleeding lip. As soon as I got a whiff of the blood on his breath, I knew, he was the one.

I pointed to my house across the street, inviting him in to clean up while he called the emergency dentist. It was the least I could do.

Ushering him into the bathroom, I had him perch on the edge of the bath while I rummaged through the cabinet for the first aid kit and tried to come up with a plan. I hadn't really thought this far ahead, but now that I had him here, I wasn't giving him up. I needed to knock him out somehow. My birdlike arms would be no match for his long, lean muscles, so I couldn't just go straight in for the kill. Unless…

Chapter Seven

"I NEED YOUR HELP." The desperation in my voice wasn't something I was proud of. A muffled moan came from behind me, and I covered the phone with my hand. "Shhh!"

"Piper? What's going on?"

"Uuummm. I did something I shouldn't have." Bringing my thumb up to my mouth, I began to chew on the corner of my nail, squinting in anticipation of his reaction.

"What did you do?" There was a rustling sound followed by a door opening and closing.

"I'm sorry," I blurted. "I know you said to be patient, but I couldn't help it."

His sigh was long and drawn out. "Where are you?"

"At home."

"Address, Piper?"

"Oh, 81 Willowby Terrace. White picket fence and bright blue door. You can't miss it."

"I'll be over in five. Don't. Do. Anything."

"Mmhmm."

"I mean it, Piper. Not a thing." The phone went silent, and I was left pacing the length of my bedroom while I waited for Mark. Running Man, as I'd so aptly named him, was curled in a twisted foetal position on my bed, his arms still tied to the headboard, but his legs pulled up to his chest. His skin had taken on a grey tinge, and it was getting greyer by the second. The pool of blood surrounding him seemed to grow larger with every beat of his heart.

I'm never going to get that stain out of my duvet.

I hadn't meant for it to go this way. I thought it would be easy, like last night, but it turned out to be a whole different ballgame. I'd taken a chance, licking the blood from his lips, quietly suggesting that I could make him feel better if we moved to my bedroom. It hadn't taken much to convince him to let me tie him up; the promise of a blow job with no strings attached too good to pass up. That was where it all went wrong.

"I'm sorry," I whispered for the tenth time. His lips moved around the balled-up rag I'd shoved in his mouth, but no sound came out. Sweat covered his face and body, and the monster inside of me wanted to lick it off. Would it taste as sweet as his blood had in my mouth?

A pounding on the door had my heart leaping into my throat. "Piper?" It was Mark, and he sounded worried. I scurried down the hall, sweeping my hair back and off my face. I'd barely unlocked the door before he barged through. "Where is he?" he asked, his eyes searching behind me.

I hooked my thumb over my shoulder. "Down there."

He stalked towards my room, his brow furrowed. I held back, not sure if I should follow. When he reached the door, he turned to face me. "You coming?"

"Mmhmm." I tucked my head into my chest and scampered down the hall. Squeezing between him and the door, I peered up at him, trying to gauge how angry he was. "I—"

He held his hand up to silence me. "Not now." Reaching over my head, he pushed, and the door swung open, revealing the mess I'd made. "Shit, Piper," he hissed. "What did you do?"

Running Man's eyes were wide, his pupils dilated and the whites turning yellow. His body shook with pain, or perhaps fear at what was coming next. As we stepped into the room, he tried to push back further against the headboard, but there was nowhere else he could go. His eyes flitted back and forth between me and Mark, his breath coming out in short, sharp pants. It didn't look good, I knew that.

"He was bleeding." I lifted my hand to my lips in explanation. "We collided." Mark quirked an eyebrow, as if he didn't believe me. "I only wanted a taste. It just took over me… the need. I thought I could recreate what we did last night."

"What we did last night? You mean you tried to bite his dick off?" He smirked, raking a hand through his hair. "I have to say, I'm a little impressed."

"I'm glad someone is. He clearly isn't." I waved my hand at Running Man. "I didn't mean to cause him so much pain. I mean, I knew it would hurt, obviously, but I thought he'd go into shock like last time, but he didn't. And, well… you'd better have a look."

"I can already guess. It wasn't a clean cut, was it?"

"No." I shook my head, inching closer to the bed. "I tried to fix it, but he's too strong. I didn't tie his legs up…"

"Amateur. Now do you understand why I asked you to wait?" He grabbed Running Man's ankles and gave a yank, stretching his legs to the end of the bed. "Get me something to tie him with." His muscles rippled with the effort it took to hold the bucking man down. Even with all his blood loss, he was still fighting to the very end, clinging onto the hope that he could make it. A tiny pang of regret weaselled its way into my heart, but even so, I knew there would be others.

With my robe sash and a belt holding Running Man's ankles in place, Mark inspected my butchering. "I couldn't get all the way through."

"I can see that." He lifted the almost-severed end of Running Man's cock with his finger. "What about this?" He pointed at the small slashes around his pelvis.

"Like I said, I tried to fix it, but he kept moving."

"This isn't how I like to do things, Piper." He pulled a blade from his back pocket with a shake of his head. "There's a reason I do it the way that I do." Pinching my chin between his thumb and forefinger, he tilted my head up to meet his gaze. "I'm trying to teach you." Without taking his eyes from me, he flicked his wrist, the blade piercing Running Man's throat, slicing all the way across in one clean sweep. His eyes widened briefly while bubbles of blood sputtered out around the rag in his mouth, and a steady stream of red poured from his throat. I couldn't tear my eyes away from the gruesome scene. It was unnerving how acclimatised I'd become already. "We'll have to wait until the cover of dark before we move him."

"Move him?"

"Yes. You're not set up here. We'll have to take him back to my place and finish it properly." My stomach tied in knots at the thought of carrying a body out of the house where anyone could see us. I didn't like it.

"I thought, maybe, I could just keep him here." I toyed with the rough edge of my nail, not wanting to meet his eyes.

"You think you can eat someone twice your size before he starts to decompose? Don't be so silly." He started untying the bonds that held Running Man down, clearly dismissing me. I'd asked him for help, not to be treated like a child. A burning need to show him I wasn't as useless as he thought, began to bubble up inside. From this night on, I would do this on my own. I wouldn't ask him for his help again.

Chapter Eight

Monday, 9th September, 2019

THE LIBRARIAN SMILED as she opened the heavy wooden door to the local public library at nine on the dot. I was among three other eager beavers to enter the silent sanctuary, and I'd already chosen the one who would occupy my thoughts for the day.

She was a petite brunette with supple skin and lonely eyes. There was an air about her, something that told me she was used to being overlooked. That was a quality I was sure I could use to my advantage. But before I could contemplate what I would do with her, I needed to do my homework.

Mark's disapproving stare and condescending attitude last night had weighed heavy on my shoulders, and I was determined to do this without his watchful eye. After all, what he didn't know, wouldn't hurt him.

Trailing my finger along the shelves of medical texts, I searched for something to help me learn the inner workings of the human body. I needed a failsafe way to end lives with as little damage as possible, and as little mess. Mark had one thing right; I wasn't set up for this kind of lifestyle in my modern townhouse, so I'd just have to get creative. No more bringing them back to my house, and certainly no more misjudged bites.

With an armload of books, I sat at one of the study tables to the rear of the library. Having taken the day off work for "women's problems" I didn't want to risk being seen by anyone. The woman I'd spied earlier was within viewing distance, but not so close she would notice. It seemed I wasn't the only one in hiding as she'd chosen to curl up on the couch in the far back corner lit only by the beam of sunlight coming through a small window above.

I found my eyes drawn to her between chapters. The way she kept brushing her hair behind her ear and nibbling her lip was mesmerising. I had to keep reminding myself of the job at hand. You have to walk before you can run. I learned that the hard way, and I wasn't about to make the same mistake twice.

***

IT WAS LATE IN THE AFTERNOON before she got up to leave, and by that time, I was ready to call it a night myself. Words were beginning to blur in front of me, and I could barely make out the notes I'd been scribbling. Closing the thick journal, I leant back in my chair, stretching my arms above my head. I'd forgotten how tiring studying could be. With any luck, I would have enough information scrawled down to come up with some semblance of a plan. Heck, at this rate, I'd settle for a rough outline. It'd been 24 hours since I'd had a feed of fresh blood, and I was desperate for a taste.

I gathered up my collection of books and stood, chancing another glance in her direction. Licking my lips, I contemplated approaching her. Her soft skin glowed under the dim lights, and all I could think about was tasting her. She stood, slinging her bag over her shoulder and brushing her hair behind her ear again. A quick glance in my direction and the smallest hint of a smile graced her lips before she walked down the aisle towards the counter. I'd missed my chance.

Shelving my books, an idea popped into my head, and I made a beeline for the fiction section. I don't know why I hadn't thought of it before. What better place to get ideas than from people who write the thing of nightmares for a living? There was bound to be something of use in one of those gore-filled horror novels people were so fond of.

As much as I'd like to think I could devour an entire human in one night, it just wasn't possible, and therein lay the problem; how do I dispose of a body without being caught?

Chapter Nine

Wednesday, 11ᵗʰ September, 2019

"OH, GOOD CHOICE. Lily Archer is one of my favourite authors." I motioned to the empty space beside her. "May I?"

She scooted aside with a shy smile. "Of course."

"Piper." I held my hand out for her and she took it.

"Mary." Her gaze fell on the cover of my Cyan Tayse book and her cheeks coloured as she ducked her head, just as I knew they would. "That's a good one also."

"Yeah? Thought I'd branch out a little and try something different." I leaned in close enough to get a whiff of her perfume. "I've always found women attractive, but I've never actually been with one before, you know?" I held the book up and wiggled it in the air. "Living vicariously." I opened the front page, waiting for her to make the next move. I'd been watching her the past few days, and she always kept to herself, but when she was reading, she blossomed like a flower, opening up and shining brightly. It almost seemed a shame to snuff out that light, but it'd been a few days since I'd had a fresh feed, and I couldn't put it off any longer.

"Oh." She giggled, flicking her hair behind her ear. "Why haven't you, um, you know, tried it?"

I shrugged, leaning back on the couch. "I don't know. I guess I never met anyone I wanted to try with. I mean, how do you even tell if a woman is straight or not? It's not like they wear a neon flashing light that says 'I'm a lesbian'." I grinned, turning back to my book. "Maybe I'll get some pointers in here though, eh?"

She giggled again, bringing her knee up to rest on the couch as she turned to face me. "You could just ask, you know? I mean, how do you tell if a man is straight?" She shrugged. "It's all the same."

I quirked a brow. "Are *you* a lesbian?"

Ducking her head down, she toyed with the hem of her top. "No… but…" She hesitated, her teeth worrying her bottom lip before meeting my gaze. "I've always wanted to try too."

Bingo.

"You have?"

She nodded. "Ever since I was in high school. I had a crush on my math teacher, Miss Fallowfield."

I pressed a hand to my chest. "It was a drama teacher for me, Miss McKenzie." I sighed wistfully. "She had the longest legs you've ever seen, and I always wondered what it would be like to have them wrapped around me." Closing the book, I set it down beside me and spun to face her. "This is probably crazy, but do you wanna get outta here? We could…" I peered behind me before leaning in close. "…explore our fantasies together."

Her eyes flicked between mine as she warred with herself. I slid my hand slowly up her thigh as I inched closer on the couch. "Come on, live a little," I whispered. "I bet you taste so sweet." My hand inched further up, my fingers curling around to the soft part of her inner thigh.

She swallowed, closing her eyes with a groan, and I knew I had her. "Okay," she whispered back.

***

UNLOCKING THE DOOR TO HER APARTMENT, she looked back at me with a nervous giggle. "I've never done anything like this before."

"There's a first time for everything." I threw her a wink as I followed through the door. "Nice place you have here." And it was. Everything was crisp and white and in its rightful place. It was almost too perfect, like one of those show homes.

"Thanks. It's simple, but I like it." She rocked back and forth on her heels, her arms swinging behind her back. "I, um, don't know what we do here," she admitted with a giggle.

Taking a step in towards her, I brought my hand up to brush a hair behind her ear, cupping her jaw in the process. She pressed her cheek into the palm of my hand, closing her eyes with a hum. She looked so sweet and serene, I couldn't help but lean in and brush my lips against hers. "How about you show me to your bathroom so I can freshen up, and you can get comfortable in the bedroom?"

"O-okay," she stuttered as she opened her eyes. "This way." She waved her arm out to the side, leading me down the hall. "Here's the bathroom, and… I guess I'll be in there." She pointed to a closed door at the end. "I'll, um, leave you to it."

Ducking her head, she half ran down the hall, stopping to gaze at me as she stepped through the door.

In the bathroom, I checked my reflection, ensuring the red wig was still in place—a Halloween costume from years gone by—then dug around in my bag until I found the knife sheathed in leather. It had a thin needle-like blade with a bone handle. I'd kept it there since Monday night, after my first day of study, just in case. I surprised myself lasting this long, but after the Running Man debacle, I'd wanted to be prepared. I couldn't have a repeat performance on my conscience. Taking a life was one thing but making them suffer was an entirely different kettle of fish. That's why I'd spent the last few days at the library researching the anatomy; to find the perfect place to strike. I was certain I had it figured out now, and unfortunately for Mary, I couldn't wait any longer. She had been in the wrong place at the wrong time.

Slipping the blade down the back of my jeans, I made my way to her bedroom. The curtains had been pulled, casting a dull glow across the room as the sun tried to break through. Mary lay on the bed in nothing but her bra and panties, and even with my preference for men, I had to admit, she was stunning. Her alabaster skin looked smooth as silk, and again, I couldn't help wondering how she would taste. After all, I'd only tried men so far.

Pulling my top over my head, I threw it on the floor before stalking towards her. "You're beautiful."

"So are you." Her eyes trailed over my body as she brought her arms across her own. "I feel underdressed."

"If anything, you're overdressed," I purred, taking hold of her hands and bringing them to her sides. "Let me look at you." Her cheeks flushed and she averted her eyes, but she didn't pull away. I let my finger trail down her arm to her hip and down her thigh, much like I'd watched Mark do that first night. Her breath kicked up, and she sucked her bottom lip in between her teeth.

Sinking to my knees, I grabbed hold of her ankles and tugged until she was close enough for me to taste without a chance of her seeing my concealed weapon.

"W-what are you doing?" She lifted her head from the mattress and peered at me with those big doe eyes of hers.

"Shhh, I only want a taste. Just lie back and relax." Hooking two fingers either side of her panties, I dragged them slowly down her hips and to the floor. The moment my hands met her bare inner thighs, she whimpered, spreading her legs wide. With the flat of my tongue, I lapped softly up one thigh and across to the other. Mary lay perfectly still but for the rise and fall of her chest. She was wound so tight, I knew it wouldn't take much to tip her over the edge. With a flick of my tongue, I had my first taste of her, circling that bundle of nerves at her core languorously. The low moan that followed spurred me on, and I delved a little deeper in an open-mouthed kiss until she could no longer hold back and began rocking back and forth against my tongue, chasing her high.

"Oh God!" she cried out, her hips bucking and her hands reaching for me. "Don't stop, please, don't stop."

I wouldn't dream of it.

Increasing the pace of my tongue, I sat up higher, my fingers wrapping around the hilt of my blade in preparation. She was so close, I could feel it.

"Yes! Oh God, yes!" Her hips lifted and her legs seized around my head as she rode out her climax. I let her finish, waiting until her legs began to relax before I made my move. With the blade already in my hand, I swung up as hard as I could, hitting the soft spot below her ribcage. In and out it went, like a hot knife through butter. Mary gasped, her mouth wide as she stared at me, but it was too late. The light was already waning from her eyes, and I whispered a soft apology as I took up my spot beside her, the heady scent of her blood beckoning me like only it could. With one final kiss to her lips, I latched onto the small hole in her side to lap up the liquid gold before it went to waste.

Once her body was drained, and I'd taken a few slices of flesh for later, I dragged her lifeless body to the bathtub I'd spied earlier. Hefting her limb by limb into the tub of hot water, I took the lye from my purse and sprinkled it in before setting the timer on my phone and closing the door. I went to work scrubbing the floor and removing the sheets from her bed, making sure there were no traces of my presence, and when I went back into the bathroom, Mary was no longer.

Chapter Ten

Monday, 16th September, 2019

LOCAL WOMAN MISSING. The bold headline caught my eye as I walked past the newsstand on my way to work. Throwing a few dollars down on the counter, I grabbed a copy and skimmed the article outlining the mysterious disappearance of Mary Blithe.

Local Woman Missing

According to family, Mary Blithe was a bit of a homebody who never ventured further than the local library. Plagued with depression and anxiety most of her adult life, her family fear for her safety. She was last seen leaving the public library on Wednesday evening with a buxom redhead. She has made no contact with anyone since, and police ask the public to come forward with any information they may have regarding her disappearance.

The tiniest hint of sadness and guilt washed over me at what I had done, but not enough to make me stop. No. I had a taste for it now, and I knew without a doubt, I'd be feeding again tonight. Mary had been but a tester, a practise of my skill, and now that I had it down pat, there was no stopping me. I'd covered my tracks carefully, thanks to the works of several authors and the worldwide web. The police had no leads, and a sense of pride bloomed in my chest at how easy it had been. A real-life *Black Widow* now roamed the streets of this sleepy town, and I'd be damned if I'd let them catch me.

Chapter Eleven

Friday, 27th September, 2019

I CROUCHED LOW in the dark alley, watching the intoxicated patrons walk past on their way to the next bar. It was only a matter of time before one lone straggler would come my way, and then, I'd have him.

My hand reached for the blade strapped to my calf, the cool metal hilt giving me a sense of comfort. Over the past few weeks I'd perfected my game, never once having to ask Mark for his assistance. I'd still been a frequent visitor at his place, soaking up any knowledge he had to bestow upon me, but ultimately, this was my calling. He would never understand my need to kill daily. That thirst that remained unquenched until I had taken another life. Fresh blood was like an aphrodisiac to me. It coursed through my body, giving me an orgasmic feeling of euphoria and strength. It was unlike anything I'd ever felt before, and there was no way I could stop it now. I had to have it.

With the last few groups having gone past already, I stood up, smoothing my top. It was time to feed.

Stepping out into the light, I leaned against the corner of the building, waiting for Mr Right. I knew him as soon as I saw him. Young and lean, just the way I liked them. He shuffled through the door, a cigarette at the ready. It wasn't my favourite flavour, but beggars can't be choosers, and his blood would still taste as sweet.

I pushed off from the wall, making myself wobble towards him, giggling as if I'd had a few too many drinks. When I was close enough, I deliberately stumbled into him, clutching his bicep.

"Woah, you okay?" He grinned, an arm snaking around my back to steady me.

"I am now, big boy." I giggled again, peering up into his crystal-blue eyes. "So strong," I gushed, giving his arm a squeeze. A little ego boost always went a long way.

He scanned the street behind me. "Are you by yourself? Do you need me to get you a cab?" His sweetness almost made me feel bad about what I was about to do.

"I don't need a cab." I walked my fingers up his chest, gazing up at him with a sultry smile. "I'm fine right here. With you." I pushed up on tip toes to catch his earlobe between my lips. The low rumble in the back of his throat made me grin as I pulled back to look up at him.

He cleared his throat, arching an eyebrow. "Is that so?"

"Mmhmm." I nodded, pulling my bottom lip in between my teeth. I let my hand trail down his chest to cup him through his pants. His tongue darted out to lick his lips as he watched me. Too easy.

"You don't beat around the bush, do you?" His voice was husky, his eyes hooded as I continued to stroke him.

"Nope." I pressed myself against him, nuzzling into his neck. "Let's go somewhere more private," I whispered. Pulling back, I waited for his nod before I took his hand and led him back to the alley. We walked past the dumpster, down to the back corner where it wasn't visible from the street.

"You don't even know me. Aren't you afraid?" he asked, his calloused fingers digging into the flesh at my waist.

"Aren't *you*?" I countered with a smirk. Before he could answer, I dropped to my knees, peering up at him with a smirk.

"Oh yeah, baby." One hand reached around to clasp my hair, the other braced against the wall.

"Easy, tiger," I purred, hastily undoing his pants until I had him free. "You don't wanna go blowing your load too soon now, do you?" Wrapping my fingers around his cock, I pumped slowly, my tongue catching the bead of come on the tip.

"Jesus," he hissed, throwing his head back against the wall. "This is actually happening."

I licked from the base to the tip, before sucking as much of him into my mouth as I could.

"Holy shit!"

My tongue swirled around his shaft, taking him to the back of my throat before pulling away and then plunging back down. His moans ignited a fire inside me, and I reached down to satisfy my own aching need. My fingers circled my swollen nub, quickly bringing me to the edge of ecstasy. The anticipation of fresh flesh was a bigger turn on than anything I'd ever experienced before, and it wasn't long before I was surfing the wave of pleasure as my fingers delved deep inside.

A keening moan slipped between my lips as I ground down on my fingers, riding out the last of my orgasm, and I knew he was getting close too because his hips began to piston back and forth, ramming his cock down my throat and bringing a tear to my eyes. When he let out a low growl and his thick, salty essence ran down my throat, I quickly withdrew my fingers and reached for my trusty blade. With as much force as I could muster, I swung it up in an arc, slamming it up under his ribs and into his heart. He was gone before he even knew what hit him.

His body slumped to the ground in a heap, and I lay on top of him, lapping up every last drop of his nectar as it flowed out of his lifeless body.

Chapter Twelve

Sunday, 29th September, 2019

"I BROUGHT SOME WINE." I smiled, holding the bottle up as I walked through the door. "Mmm, something smells delicious."

Mark placed his hand on the small of my back, leading me through to the kitchen. "It should, I've been slaving away in the kitchen all afternoon." Two wine glasses were sitting on the counter at the ready. Whisking the bottle from my hands, he poured us both a hefty drink. "Are you ready to try the fruits of our labour?" He clinked his glass with mine with a grin. "I think it's one of my best yet."

"It must be my touch that gives it that extra kick." I winked, taking a sip from my glass. "What are we having?"

He held a finger in the air, placing his glass on the counter and making his way over to the pantry.

"I have a little something I prepared earlier." A plate adorned with cheese and crackers, grapes and jerky was placed in front of me. I had to admit, I was a little excited to try the meat we'd had drying from that first night.

I reached out and snaffled a hunk of meat, popping it into my mouth. "This is delicious," I mumbled, surprised at just how good it was. Something similar to pride blossomed in my chest at the thought that I'd had a hand in making such a delicacy.

"Like I said, it's all in the way you cure it." He helped himself to a piece too. "And, of course, a bit of patience." It'd been three weeks since I'd had to call him for help, but he still liked to remind me of this virtue I was lacking. I hated to think how he'd feel if he found out about my nightly kills.

"Well, it's a good thing I have you to keep me in line then, isn't it?" I would play along with his game, pretending that I hadn't outgrown the teacher. "So, what else is on the menu?"

"Ah." His eyes shone as he waved an arm toward the oven. "Come and see." He pulled the door down, grabbing a tea towel to save his hands from the heat as he tugged the tray out. "Leg roast with rosemary and garlic potatoes." He placed the tray on top of the oven, ladling the juices over the meat. "It's almost done." The rich aroma had me salivating. It wasn't fresh meat, but it smelled divine all the same. "And," he swept the tray back into the oven. "I thought we could make a start on our next catch while we wait." He turned, leaning his hip against the counter and folding his arms across his chest. "I know how you like it fresh."

"That I do." I smiled, knowing what he had in mind. It had become something of a ritual on a Sunday evening. I would come over for another 'lesson' and there would be a new man tied to the bed for me to devour. It was an easier kill, less thrill, but fresh meat is fresh meat. I would never turn my nose up at it. "Lead the way."

Taking my hand, he took me down the hall, to the back of the house to where it all began. As was customary, he stopped and stared at a spot on the wall over my shoulder, his hand poised over the door handle as he took a breath. A tingle of anticipation ran through me as I waited for him to open the door. Who would it be this time?

Strapped, spread-eagle to the bed, was a muscular man who looked to be somewhere in his mid-thirties. His hair was slicked back with gel and a blindfold covered his eyes, as was the norm. At the sound of our footsteps on the hardwood floor, his head lifted from the pillow. "I-I've changed my mind," he stuttered. "I don't want this. Not anymore." I looked to Mark, wondering what he would do about it. "I promise, I won't tell anyone. Just, please, let me go." His head kept flicking from left to right, trying to reason with the enemy he couldn't see.

With a sigh, Mark glanced to the side before shaking his head. "I can't do that." He stood over him, exuding a power that he kept well-hidden most of the time. I liked this side of him; so different to the man I met in the supermarket all those weeks ago.

"P-please!"

"It's too late. We can't take any chances. I'm sorry." His cleaver swung down, slicing from sternum to navel. A sharp cry burst from our man before his head lolled to the side. Blood teemed from the incision, coating the sheets. The intoxicating scent filled my nostrils, eliciting a groan. I couldn't stop myself. I dove on top of his body, burying my face in the open wound, lapping up every bit I could.

Mark's hand clamped down on my shoulder. "I'm sorry, Piper. That wasn't how it was meant to go. I thought you could play with him a little first."

Coming up for air, I turned my bloodied face to him. "No need to apologise." I grinned, having no doubt that there would be tissue hanging from between my teeth. "Fresh is best, no matter how you do it."

Chapter Thirteen

Friday, 4ᵗʰ October, 2019

I FASTENED THE SHEATH to my leg, making sure it was good and tight before sliding my knife inside. It was my favourite time of day. Hunting time. The thrill still hadn't worn off, and I hoped it never would.

In the bathroom, I stood in front of the mirror, applying my mascara and a slather of lippy before pulling my hair up into a messy bun. My little black dress slipped over my head, falling into place over my lacy underwear. The last thing to go on was my black stiletto-heeled fuck-me boots; the perfect way to conceal my weapon, and another part of the ruse. If you're going to do something, you may as well go the whole hog and look the part.

Out on the street, I strutted my way into town, keeping my eyes peeled for my next victim. I was in the mood for someone with a bit more meat on their bones. So far, my pickings hadn't varied much, but I wanted to branch out, try new things.

It wasn't long before I spotted him. The brooding lone wolf. Yes, he would do nicely.

He was tall but not willowy. His jet-black hair fell around his face, framing his brilliant green eyes. Dressed in jeans that clung to his thick thighs, and a tight, white tee, it was plain to see he was ripped. He would be stronger than me, but I liked a challenge.

Crossing the road, I put as much swing into my hips as I could without falling over. I didn't have to look to know he was watching me. I could practically feel his eyes raking over my body. This one was going to be fun.

"Excuse me," I breathed, pulling my lip in between my teeth and tipping my head to the side. "Are you… Brad?" I dipped my eyes, giving the impression I was embarrassed.

"No, but I wish I was." He looked me up and down, his eyes lingering on the full swell of my breasts. I arched my back, pushing them out even further.

"Oh, that's too bad. I was meant to be meeting him here." I giggled, peering up at him sheepishly. "Blind date."

His eyebrows shot up. "*You're* on a blind date?"

I shrugged. "I'm meant to be." I looked around. "I think maybe I've been stood up though."

"His loss." Shoving his hands in his pockets, he coughed to clear his throat. "Uh, I'll take you out. If you want."

I beamed up at him. *Got him.* "Really? You'd do that for me?"

"Are you kidding? You're a knock-out. The guy who stood you up needs his head read." He shook his head in disbelief.

"Well, you have just made my night." Placing my hands on his broad chest, I stretched up and kissed his cheek. "Thank you."

"I'd be an even bigger fool than him if I left you standing here by yourself." He smiled, his perfectly plump lips stretching wide. "So, what would you like to do?"

With a flutter of my lashes, I said, "You want to come back to my place?"

****

FOR SOMEONE WHO'D AVOIDED MEN like the plague for several years, I found it surprisingly easy to jump back into the groove of things. Mark had given me a new kind of freedom. A new way of living, and I was embracing it with everything in my being. I liked this new, self-assured Piper. I liked that I could bend men to my will with only the bat of an eye. And Josh was no different to the rest of them. He'd buckled like a new-born foal taking its first steps.

He was stronger than the rest, and judging by the bulge in his pants, he was packing more too. I couldn't wait to sink my teeth into him, literally, but I had another itch that needed scratching first. An itch that only he could help me with.

I played the old "oops, I dropped something" trick, bending over in front of him, giving him an eyeful of my lace panties. His growl sent a jolt straight to my core.

Straightening up, I spun around to see him stalking towards me. Anticipating his move, I pounced, wrapping my legs around his waist as our lips collided. His calloused hands cupped my ass, grinding me against his growing hardness. I didn't even have to pretend when I moaned into his mouth. I wanted him inside me, in more ways than one.

He carried me to the counter, setting me down on the cool stone so he could shuck off his tee. My dress was next to go, and he stood, raking his eyes over my body in appreciation. "Brad doesn't know what he's missing." He shook his head with a grin. His hands slid up my thighs, roaming my curves as he pulled me into him. I rocked my hips, anxious to feel him against me. With one hand, he unzipped his jeans, pushing them over his hips along with his boxers. Gripping his shaft, he rubbed the tip over my soaking panties before pulling the fabric to the side and plunging deep inside.

I swear my eyes rolled to the back of my head; it was that intense. His fingers dug into my hips as he thrust into me, each time feeling even better than the last, until I was climbing that high, seeking my ecstasy, and Josh was right there with me. Our tongues warred with each other while our hands tried to touch every last bit of flesh, as if we couldn't get enough.

I was clinging to the edge, desperate to fall, and when he pressed his thumb to my clit, I did. I fell so hard I could see stars. I clung to his shoulders, holding on for dear life as I came down from my high, waiting for my moment.

"Fuck!" he roared, slamming into me one last time. I coiled around him, my hand fumbling inside my boots. When my fingers found purchase on the blade, I yanked it out and up under his ribs in my signature move. He barely had a chance to realise what had happened before he slid out of my grip and onto the floor.

Jumping off the counter, I straddled his waist, his cock nestled between my thighs. My fingers skirted over his wound, blood coating them. I had to taste him. Bringing my hand to my mouth, I stuck out my tongue, lapping up the sweet juices. With a groan, I dropped down, sealing my lips over the hole in his side. I sucked and licked until there was nothing left, just the empty shell of a man.

Chapter Fourteen

"IT'S YOU, ISN'T IT? The one who's responsible for all the missing men?" His eyes flashed with anger as he thrust the local paper in my face.

"And hello to you too."

"Piper?" He clenched his jaw, the vein in his forehead popping out.

"So what if it is?" I waved my hand dismissively as I snatched the paper from his hands, skimming the article with a snort. "They haven't even got the number right, and they weren't all men." I flicked the paper on the table as I walked past. "They'll never catch me." I carried on down the hall to our lair with all the arrogance of a practised killer. Regardless of the fact he was yelling at me, I knew what would be waiting for me; it was Sunday night. It was what we did.

"You don't know that!" He stalked behind me, swiping the paper off the table and rustling it in the air. "They'll figure it out, it's only a matter of time."

"You're just upset that I'm better at this than you. I've got it down to an art now. I'm telling you, they won't catch me."

"You're being reckless. One day, you'll slip up and it'll be all over, and for what? We have more than enough to last us here."

I stopped, facing him with a shake of my head. "No, it's *not* enough for me. I crave the *fresh* meat, the *warm* blood, that's what gets me going. Not this…" I waved my hand through the air, "…dried meat in your cold store."

"I bring you a fresh kill every week!"

"I need more than that! Once a week isn't enough!"

His shoulders sagged as he rubbed a hand down his face. He looked tired. "Piper, you can't keep doing this."

"Why? Why can't I?"

"Because!"

"Because? That's not an answer. Need I remind you, you're the one who introduced me to this life? You can't give it and then take it away. I have a taste for it now."

"You think I don't know that? I don't wanna take it away from you, but I have to. Someone has to be the voice of reason, and that someone is me. You can't keep doing this, Piper."

"Give me one good reason why."

"Because…" He raked a hand through his hair. "Because I've only just found you, okay? It's just been me for so long, and now that I have you, I can't lose you." He paused. "This thing we have between us?" He pointed at me and then himself. "It's come to mean a lot to me. More than I think you realise. I don't think I can let you go."

His heartfelt words hit me like a slap to the face, and suddenly it all made sense. His cautions, his rules, they were all to protect me. To protect *us*. He wanted a future with me.

I smoothed my hands up his chest, lacing my fingers around his neck. He watched me, silently waiting for me to make the first move. I stepped into him, inhaling his musky scent as I ran my tongue along the crook of his neck and up to his ear. A little nibble on his soft flesh had him groaning, and when I pulled back, our lips crashed together as he pushed me up against the wall. His hands curved around my face and into my hair, tugging forcefully. I tilted my head, giving him the access he desired.

"God, I've wanted you for so long." His voice was husky, filled with need. Sliding his hands down my back, he cupped my arse, lifting me into his arms. When he discovered my sheer panties, he ripped them off me with a growl. I rocked my hips against him as he carried me to the bed, lowering me down. "Let's get these off." He grabbed hold of my stiletto boot.

"No." I reached down to touch myself and draw his attention away. "Leave them on." With one hand rubbing circles on my clit, I beckoned him closer with the other. "Taste," I whispered, placing my fingers in his mouth.

"Mmm." He crawled up my body, his lips finding mine once more. I bit down on his bottom lip, getting that taste I needed. I wrapped my legs around his waist and twisted, pushing him onto his back. His pants were already undone, and I didn't bother pulling them all the way down, just enough to get him out to play. With a few quick pumps of my hand, I could tell he was more than ready for me. Keeping my eyes locked onto his, I lowered myself down, his cock filling me. He grabbed hold of my hips, setting the pace as he rocked me back and forth in a frenzy. This moment had been building for so long, neither of us could hold back any longer.

He closed his eyes, throwing his head back with a roar as he came. Without a second thought, I unsheathed the knife I kept strapped to my calf, and with one sweep, stuck it deep under his ribcage. "Now you'll never have to let me go," I whispered, leaning down to lap up the warm crimson nectar flowing from his wound. Having had my fill, I pulled back to see the hint of a smile gracing his lips. I took pleasure in knowing I had given him what he wanted in his final moments.

As I walked down the hallway, his blood coating my lips, something caught my eye. It was the puzzle we'd started and not finished all those nights ago. With no real need to hurry, I settled on the couch and started slotting the pieces in. The picture began to take shape. It was a dark room with a couch much like the one I was sitting on, and behind it was a woman dressed in grey. Her hair was pulled back in a tight bun and the smirk on her face was eerie. But it was her eyes that caught my attention. They seemed... familiar, as if I'd seen them before.

A cool breeze blew in from the window behind me, sending a chill down my spine. It was then that I felt it. Another presence in the room. I stood slowly, my body tense as tiny step by tiny step, I turned around. A blood-curdling scream tore from my throat as I came face to face with the woman from the picture.

She walked around the couch, her hands clasped behind her back, and that damn smirk on her face. Frozen to the spot, I could do nothing but follow her with my eyes as my heart thundered in my chest. Who was she, and why was she here?

She stood directly in front of me, her wrinkled eyes taking me in. Her lips brushed my ear as she leaned in, whispering those familiar words, "Gluttony is a sin." And before I could register the movement, she brought her arm up, plunging a knife into my side. Not a killshot like I'd perfected, but enough to slow me down. My hand automatically flew to the wound, trying to staunch the flow of blood as it oozed out.

"All my boy wanted was someone else to share this with, but instead, he created another monster." A searing pain ripped up my other side as she stabbed me again. "Someone worse than him. Always wanting more. Never satisfied. Even now, all you can think about is what your own blood would taste like."

She was right. It was sick and twisted, but the coppery smell was like an addiction. One whiff and I had to have it, even if it was my own. But how could she possibly know that?

It took a minute for her words to sink in. *Her boy*. "He was… he was your son?" I staggered backwards, reaching for the couch to steady me. "You knew? What he did? What *we* did?"

She threw her head back and laughed, reminding me of the boyish way Mark had done the same thing, only this was much more sinister. "Of course I knew! Who do you think taught him? He sure as hell didn't come up with it on his own." She shook her head, using the blade as a finger as she pointed at her own head. "A mother always knows when her son is different. He just needed a bit of guidance, to be taught self-control, to heed the seven sins." She circled around me like a tiger and its prey. "I knew as soon as he brought you here, you'd be trouble, but he wouldn't listen. Desperate to have someone other than dear old Mum to share his perversions with."

Twisting my head to keep watch of her, I couldn't hide the confusion.

"Oh, you didn't know I was watching you? Not so clever now, are you, deary?"

The hairs on the back of my neck stood on end as I realised what or *who* he'd been looking at all those times he'd led me down the hallway. "No." I shook my head. "I don't believe you. You can't have been watching this whole time."

"Oh but I have. Mark was a real Mummy's boy, you know? Didn't really get on with a lot of people. Not even his daddy. Not until you. And then you went and hurt him just like all the others. Only this time, he can't bounce back, can he, Piper?"

"I-I'm sorry," I stuttered, the pain making me feel woozy.

"Sorry doesn't bring him back." She ripped my shirt open, the buttons flying across the room. The cool tip of her blade ran across my exposed skin. "You should have listened to him that first night." She pressed harder, and I could feel the blood trickle down my chest. "Gluttony. Is. A. Sin." As she spoke each word, she sliced into my flesh with an agonising precision. Not deep enough to kill, just enough to cause pain.

Dipping her head to my chest, she trailed her tongue over the gashes she'd created, sending a jolt of pleasure and pain through me. "Mmm, it's been a long time since I've had a fresh feed." She licked her lips, my blood smeared across her face. "I guess that's one thing we have in common. Fresh is best." Her mouth slammed into mine, and I was hit with a kind of euphoria at the taste of my own blood on my lips. "How does it taste?" she whispered before thrusting the blade up under my ribs as I'd done to Mark mere moments before. Only she wasn't as practised as I was, missing my heart and hitting my lungs instead.

Blood bubbled up from inside, filling my mouth. And even as I felt my life slip away, I revelled in the scent and taste I'd come to love so much. Gluttony really *was* a sin, one that needed to be put to rest. Swallowing what I could, I ran my tongue along my bottom lip and grinned at her. "Almost… as good… as you." Mustering the last of my strength, I lunged, sinking my teeth into her throat.

Her garbled cry rang in my ears as we crumpled in a heap on the floor. The Mother and the Whore entwined in a pool of blood. The word GLUTTON carved into my skin in a silent admission of our sins.

A Note from the Author

Thank you so much for reading *Sins of the Flesh*. If you enjoyed reading it, please do leave a review as they help other readers find it, and they allow us to better our skill.

Sins of the Flesh was originally part of the *Witching Hour, Vices and Virtues anthology*, and it was the first time I branched out into something a little different. I have to say, I quite enjoy the darker side of writing!

Other Books by Stacey Broadbent

Hollywood novel
Emma

Standalone
Never Judge a Book

A Step in Time series
Dancing through the Storm
Dancing in Circles
Dancing with Destiny
A Step in Time: the complete series

Super Mum series
Super Mum? From one frazzled mum to another
Super Mum! Frazzled, Frumpy and Fabulous!
Super Mum, Fighting fit (but still frazzled)
Super Mum box set (books 1-3)

Flesh-eater series
Fear the Fever
Fight the Fever

Anthologies
A Touch of Inspiration
Key to my Heart
Scars to your Beautiful
Witching Hour: Vices and Virtues
The White Ribbon Collection

About the Author

Stacey lives in Ashburton, New Zealand, with her husband and three children. An avid reader and self-confessed book-a-holic, she has always had a love of the written word, so it was only a matter of time before she took pen to paper and began on her writing journey.

Stacey is a multi-genre author, with books from light-hearted comedies to zombie thrillers to contemporary romance. You can often find her lurking on social media so don't be afraid to reach out and have a chat.

http://www.staceybroadbent.weebly.com
https://www.facebook.com/StaceyBroadbentAuthor
Broadbent's Bookish Babes: https://goo.gl/FY9wQN
Goodreads: https://goo.gl/YJ6dXa
https://www.instagram.com/authorstaceybroadbent/
https://www.bookbub.com/authors/stacey-broadbent
https://www.pinterest.nz/authorstaceybroadbent/
Newsletter sign-up: http://eepurl.com/cULu_f
Arc Team: https://goo.gl/J5Tf6s